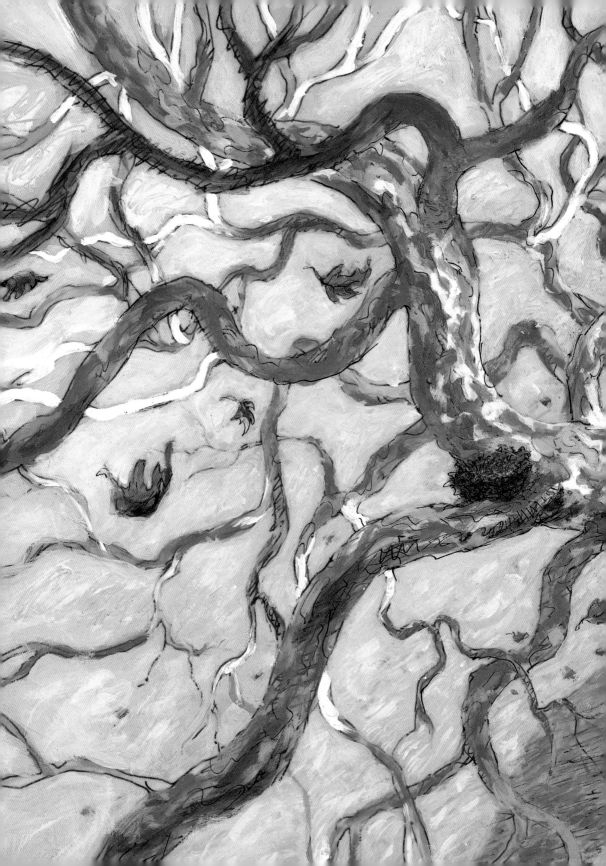

Albert
and the Angels

Leslie Norris

Pictures by

Mordicai Gerstein

Farrar, Straus and Giroux
New York

ALBERT WAS HAPPY. He was sitting on a bench beneath the sycamore tree, thinking deep thoughts. He liked thinking deep thoughts better than anything.

"Lucille," he said to his dog, "I believe it is getting colder. We must make a note of that."

Lucille was a very small dachshund. "It's been getting colder for weeks," she said. "Have you been asleep?"

"I sometimes wish," said Albert, "that you weren't able to speak. You are often quite rude."

"Since you're the only person who can hear me," said Lucille, "it doesn't matter if I'm rude. Go on about the cold."

It was true that only Albert could hear what Lucille said.

"All the leaves have fallen," said Albert, "except the last one on this sycamore. Do you know what the date is?"

"I have no idea," said Lucille. "I know when it is hot and when it is cold. Today is quite chilly."

"Today is December the first," Albert said. "Make a note of that. It will soon be Christmas."

"Make a note, make a note," Lucille said. "You know I can't write."

The last leaf fell from the sycamore tree. It spun and drifted through the air and landed red as sunset on the grass. Albert and Lucille looked at the leaf.

"It's exactly the color of your hair," said Albert.

"And yours," Lucille said.

And so it was. They smiled at each other.

"Now it is really winter," Albert said.

Lucille kicked up her legs.

Together they went indoors.

Albert stood in the kitchen, leaning against the counter. "I don't like my name," he said to his mother. "Albert. What a terrible name."

His mother was preparing supper. There was a marvelous smell in the house. "Don't you?" she said. "I like it. I think it's good, very dignified. It means you will achieve great things. There was a king of Belgium named Albert."

"There was?" said Albert. "I bet he's dead."

"Well," said his mother, "that was a long time ago. Anyway, it was your grandfather's name. He was a fine man. He was pleased that we named you after him."

Albert could not remember his grandfather. "It will soon be Christmas," he said. He thought of all the presents he would have.

"Mom," he said, "what was the best Christmas present you ever got?"

His mother stopped rattling the dishes. "That's easy," she said. "When I was your age, eight years old, my grandmother gave me a medallion. It was round and made of gold, and it hung from a delicate gold chain. Oh, I loved it."

"I've never seen it," Albert said. "What did it look like?"

"There was a tree," his mother said, "a Christmas tree, on the face of the medallion. And my birth date, September 24, 1922, was engraved on the back along with my name, Helen Lavinia O'Keefe."

"That is your middle name?" said Albert. "Lavinia? I didn't know that. It's as bad as Albert. I thought your name was just Helen."

"I like Lavinia," his mother said. "It was my grandmother's name."

"Where is the medallion now?" Albert asked.

His mother looked sad. "Lost." She sighed. "I lost it

years ago. I've no idea where I lost it. It just vanished. I wish I could find it again."

"So do I," said Albert.

That night, as he lay in bed, Albert had a deep thought. "Lucille," he said, "Mom really liked that medallion."

"Keep your feet still," said Lucille. "I am asleep."

"Do you think we could find it for her?" Albert asked.

"Very unlikely," Lucille answered. "Perhaps we could buy one like it. You could save your money."

"I can't hope to save any by Christmas," said Albert. "I wish my father would give me more allowance."

"Perhaps," said Lucille, "you should tell your father to give me an allowance, too."

"Oh yes," said Albert. "What would you do with an allowance?"

"I'd lend it to you," replied Lucille. "You could pay me back a little each week."

"You are not very amusing, Lucille," Albert said.

Try as he might, Albert could not earn any extra money. Every day he offered to run errands and wash the dinner dishes.

His parents were surprised. "What has happened to our boy?" his father said. "Is he getting sick?"

"I'm fine," Albert said. "I just like being helpful." He did not want to ask for money—and he did not get any.

Sooner than Albert had thought possible, it was Christmas Eve. He counted his money. He counted it fifteen times, and it was always the same. It was eighty-three cents and a foreign coin.

"It's no good," he told Lucille. "We can't do it. We don't have nearly enough to buy a gold medallion on a delicate gold chain. We're beaten."

Lucille licked his ear. "That's sad," she said, "because we've tried so hard to get enough money."

"I'm very unhappy," Albert said.

"I can understand that," said Lucille. She nestled closer to Albert. "Why don't we," she said, "to comfort ourselves in our sadness, buy some candy? We have plenty of money for that."

Lucille was fond of candy, although she wasn't supposed to eat any. It upset her stomach.

"Oh, all right," said Albert. "Just one bar."

They walked down to the store. The day was dreary. Black clouds rolled about in the sky, and the wind whipped and huffed.

Albert bought one bar of candy. It was called a Big Hunk. It cost ten cents. They ate it on the way home. "Now we have only seventy-three cents," Albert said.

Albert and Lucille sat in Albert's bedroom. Albert looked at his photographs of lions and elephants, as straight as soldiers on the shelves, and he sighed. "I'm sorry we ate that candy," he said.

"*We* didn't eat it," Lucille said. "That was hardly fifty-fifty. You ate nearly all of it."

"If you compare our sizes," said Albert, "you did very well. You should have had less than a hundredth part of what I had."

"I did have less than a hundredth part," said Lucille nastily. "I needed perfect eyesight to find what you gave me. If I were a rottweiler, you wouldn't have had anything. I should have eaten it all."

"I feel terrible that we ate it," said Albert. "We should have kept our money."

"That is true," said Lucille. "We have been selfish."

Albert took up his flute and began to play.

"You always play beautifully," Lucille said, "but the music is sad."

"It helps me," said Albert. "It's instead of crying."

"You play very well indeed," Lucille said. "Well enough to give a concert."

Albert put down the flute. He began to smile. His eyes shone. "Lucille," he said, "you are a genius. You are brilliant."

"Anytime," said Lucille modestly. "It's no trouble."

Albert and Lucille stood on the corner of Main Street. All around them, the windows of the Christmas stores were bright with shining and expensive presents. A cold wind blew from the east, and the streets were filling with evening.

Albert took his flute from its case and polished it on his sleeve. Men and women were hurrying home from their offices, some doing their final shopping and tugging small children along behind them. Everywhere, people scurried around Albert and Lucille.

Albert blew a quiet note. He could scarcely hear it. "Here goes, Lucille," he said. As clearly and confidently as he could, he began to play "Good King Wenceslas."

Lucille sat up and begged. She didn't beg well, because she was shivering with cold.

Nobody paid any attention to them.

One after another, Albert played all the carols he knew.

Nothing at all happened.

Albert breathed hard on his cold fingers. "One last try," he said. But as he lifted the flute to his lips, a large policeman appeared.

"What's all this?" said the policeman.

Albert explained that he was trying to collect enough money to buy a small round medallion on a delicate gold chain. "It's for my mother," he said.

"Playing your flute in the street!" the policeman said. "What next? Don't you know it's against the law for children to play for money in the street?"

"No, sir," said Albert.

"He plays beautifully," said Lucille, but only Albert heard her.

The policeman put his hand in his pocket. "Here," he said. "I should arrest you, really. Clap you in jail. For life, I daresay. But it's Christmas Eve, after all. Take this, and go home." He gave Albert a bill.

"Yes, sir," said Albert. "Thank you, sir."

The policeman turned and marched away.

Albert and Lucille watched him leave.

"How much?" asked Lucille.

Albert unfolded the bill and looked at it. "A dollar," he said. "The policeman gave me a whole dollar."

"Good," Lucille said. "What do we do now?"

Albert picked up Lucille from the cold pavement and put her under his coat. "Now we find a shop," he said. "A jeweler's shop. We may have enough to buy a gold medallion."

The first jeweler's they went into was called Ellerby's. It was quiet there. The carpets were thick and rich. Tall clocks stood against the wall. A brilliant treasury of rings and bracelets and necklaces glittered in their glass cases.

A thin, elegant young man floated toward Albert. "Yes?" he said. "Is there some way I can help you?"

"I want a small, round medallion made of gold," said Albert, "on a delicate gold chain."

The young man sniffed in a superior way. He gazed distantly above Albert's head. "How much were you thinking of spending?" he asked.

"I have one dollar and seventy-three cents," Albert said.

"I shouldn't think . . ." began the young man. Then he looked down at Albert. He saw Lucille's head poking out of Albert's coat. "Is that a dog?" he said. "Take that animal out of the store at once. Dogs are *not* allowed in this establishment."

"She's such a small dog," protested Albert.

"I don't care if you can put her in a silver thimble," the young man said. "Out, out! At once!"

Albert and Lucille found themselves outside in the falling darkness.

"In a silver thimble, indeed!" Lucille snarled. "If you had put me down, I'd have given him silver thimble!"

Although they tried four other stores, not one could sell Albert and Lucille a gold medallion. They did not have enough money.

Albert and Lucille trudged along, not knowing what to do next. As they left Main Street, they found fewer shops. Only one store window blazed with light, a small window, full of tinsel and silver Christmas bells and trays of cheap earrings and holly. It was amazing that one small window could hold so many things.

"Let's try this one," said Lucille. "I have a good feeling about it."

They went in. There were streamers and paper decorations and stuffed animals and balloons and model cars and marionettes and every kind of doll. Kites were hanging from the ceiling. Every inch of space held some bright thing. It was warm in the store.

A blond young woman was lounging behind the counter. Her lips were scarlet. She was painting her nails. "You're late," she said. "I can't stay open forever, you know." She looked at her reflection in a mirror nearby. The frame of the mirror was covered with seashells.

Albert didn't think it was the kind of store that could possibly have what he wanted.

"Why don't you ask?" said Lucille. "You won't get anything unless you ask. And I'm cold."

Albert looked around. He saw bright baskets of glass beads, tumults of ticking toys, balloons just made for bouncing, water guns and kettledrums, piles of practical jokes, rows of radiant stars for sheriffs, bundles of brooches, bangles, necklaces, and cheap jewels of all kinds and colors. He could not see anything like a small gold medallion.

The young woman waved her scarlet nails in the air. "Well," she said, "come on. I can't wait all night. I'm off to a party as soon as you've decided what you want."

"Hoity-toity," said Lucille. "In a hurry, aren't we."

"I want a small, gold medallion on a delicate gold chain," Albert said. "It's for my mother."

"Very nice, too," the young woman said. "I may have something. Let's look."

She took a box from under the counter and rummaged about in it. "Thought so," she said. "Here's the very thing."

"How much is it?" said Albert.

"How much have you got?" the young woman asked.

"One dollar and seventy-three cents," Albert said.

"You can have it for that," the young woman said. She took the medallion out of the box and held it, hanging on its chain, in front of Albert's eyes.

It was not a small medallion. It was not round. It was not on a fine, delicate gold chain. It was on a heavy, clumsy chain. It was not made of gold. It was cheap. It was tawdry.

Albert took a deep breath. "My mother wouldn't like it," he said.

"She would," said the young woman. "I'm sure she would. In any case, it's the only one I have."

"Take it," said Lucille.

Albert thought hard.

"It's too late to look for anything else," said Lucille.

At least it was a medallion on a chain.

"I'll take it," Albert said.

The young woman wrapped it. Even the wrapping paper seemed awful. Albert paid his money.

"You won't regret it," said the young woman. She was already putting on her coat.

Albert closed the door behind him. At once, as fast as a thought, the store lights went out. Light snow began to fall through the town.

Albert and Lucille ran home through the snow.

Albert put down his flute, then took off his coat and shook it free of the clinging snow. He could see his face in the hall mirror. Snow covered his hair, so that he looked like an ancient boy.

"Look at this, Lucille," he said. "I have white hair. I could be eighty years old instead of eight."

"It's already melting," Lucille said.

"Now to examine this medallion," said Albert. He put his hand into his coat pocket.

The small package was not there. Nor was it in his other pockets. He could not find it anywhere. "Lucille," he said, "I have lost the medallion."

Dismayed, they looked at each other.

Albert was tired. He was cold. He had never been so unhappy. He felt as if he really were eighty years old.

Albert and Lucille walked slowly into the living room. The Christmas tree was covered with the tiny lights that Albert loved so much, red ones and green ones, shining like stars through the branches. His presents waited for him at the foot of the tree, but Albert did not look at them.

"Why, Albert," said his mother, "whatever is the matter? Are you ill? Look at you, you're soaking wet."

"I'm all right," said Albert. "Lucille and I have been out in the snow, that's all."

"Hmm," said his father. "You do look awful. It's all this excitement about Christmas, that's what it is."

"Off to bed with you," said Albert's mother. "We were going to sing carols together, but we can do that tomorrow. I'll bring you a hot drink."

Albert and Lucille crept miserably to bed.

But Albert didn't sleep. Even after he had drunk the hot chocolate his mother brought him, he didn't sleep.

Albert lay awake in his room. He heard his father lock the house against the night. He heard his parents make their way upstairs. He saw the lights go out. Albert listened to the comfortable sounds the house made as it settled down.

The old grandfather clock in the hall slowly measured the hours.

At two o'clock, Albert rose from his bed. He had never gotten up so early before. Making no noise, he dressed in his warmest clothes.

Carefully, he picked up the sleepy Lucille and carried her downstairs.

Albert put on his heavy boots for the coldest weather, the red wool cap that he could pull over his ears, his thick gloves. Then he tugged Lucille's knitted coat over her head and down her plump little body. He made sure her short legs went through the holes in front. She was snug and warm.

"Where are we going?" said Lucille.

"To search for the medallion," Albert answered.

"Some hope," grumbled Lucille. "But we might as well try."

Slowly Albert unlocked the door. It swung open on its silent hinges.

Cautiously, inch by inch, he closed the door behind them. Then Albert and Lucille stepped into the darkness.

Snow began to fall again, this time heavily. A strong wind blew the stinging flakes into Albert's face. He lowered his head against the gale and struggled forward.

The snow was deep enough to bury Lucille. Albert lifted her and huddled her under his jacket. The wind blew heavy drifts that covered everything. Snow was changing the world.

Albert staggered on, head down, bent forward, unable to see, pushing his aching legs against the knee-high snow. It seemed that he had been walking for hours.

Albert looked up, wiping the snow from his face with a gloved hand. He could not see more than a few yards in front of him. He did not recognize the street in which he stood, not the houses, not their dark windows, nothing. Grim and scared, he stood in the whirling storm.

"What's wrong?" Lucille asked, panting. "I can feel that something is wrong!"

"We're lost," said Albert. "We're completely lost."

Lucille wriggled inside Albert's jacket. "Press on," she said. "Keep moving. We must keep moving."

And Albert trudged on.

He was stopped short by a solid object. It was a large object, bigger than Albert. It was not hard, and it was not soft. It was firm.

Lucille jumped down. Albert raised his head and looked. It was a boy. He had walked into a boy.

"Hey," the boy said, "look where you're going. You might have done me an injury, thumping into me like that!"

"I'm sorry," said Albert. "I couldn't see you."

"Couldn't see me?" the boy said, widening his eyes. "That's a laugh. I'm big enough, aren't I? Solid enough, aren't I?"

"It was the snow," said Albert. "It was blowing so hard I kept my head down."

"You are a funny one," the boy said. "What snow? I don't feel any snow."

Sure enough, the snow had stopped. So had the wind. The sky was perfectly clear, except for a few ragged clouds that blew across the moon. The stars were scattered over the sky, glittering like frost fire.

Albert was confused. He looked at the boy. His face was round. He wore a blue jacket pulled tightly across his sturdy body. His jeans were faded.

"What are you doing here?" asked Albert. "Who are you?"

"I'm waiting for you," the boy said. "I'm one of the angels."

"An angel?" said Albert.

"One of them," the boy said. "You can call me Redvers. Now, hurry up, young Albert. We haven't got all night." He took Albert's hand in one of his and pulled Albert along.

Suddenly Albert was no longer tired. He felt warm and strong. He ran on top of the snow with Redvers, and had never felt stronger. And Lucille ran with them.

"Where are we going?" Albert cried. The speed of their running blew the breath from his mouth in a white cloud.

"You'll see," said Redvers. "It's not far now."

They ran light as leaves through the dark streets. They were in the old part of town. Albert had never been there before.

They ran down a long, narrow road, with tall houses on either side.

"Come on!" cried Redvers. "We have to hurry! Faster!"

They raced past the houses, into an open space.

"This is it," Redvers said. "We've arrived."

"What?" said Albert, disappointed. "This place? It's like an old car lot."

There was nothing there—except a shabby wooden building, unpainted, its roof sagging, its walls leaning aslant. Nothing but an old barn.

"You'll see," Redvers said.

As he spoke, the barn door opened and a brilliant light streamed out. It shone through the open door and through the gaps in the cracked walls. It lit up the snow until every fallen flake burned like silver fire. The whole vacant lot glittered and shimmered in the splendor of the light.

Out of the door stepped a man. "Welcome," he said. "Welcome, Albert. And little Lucille, welcome."

"There," said Redvers. "What do you think of that?"

Albert looked at the man. He was not young. His face was red and cheerful. He rubbed his hands briskly together. He was smiling. His glasses shone in the blazing light.

"You're here at last," he said. "Well done, Redvers, my boy. Come in. We haven't much time."

Albert walked toward the man.

A neat sign near the door said:

A. N. ANGEL
Found Property
Visits by Appointment

"Sir," said Albert. "Mr. Angel, I think I may be in the wrong place. I am looking for a medallion that I lost. The medallion is *lost* property."

"So it was," Mr. Angel said. "It was. We may say it used to be lost. Everything in my warehouse was once lost. But when it reaches me, it becomes *found* property. You see?"

"I think so," said Albert.

"Then step inside," Mr. Angel said grandly. "Please enter." He waved Albert into his brilliant, tumbledown barn. Albert stepped in.

He gasped.

The inside of the barn was enormous. It was larger than City Hall. It was larger than any airplane hangar. It was bigger than the White House. It was totally splendid.

"It gets bigger all the time," said Mr. Angel. "There is always a great deal of found property."

"Don't people come to claim it?" asked Albert.

"Only special people are invited," Mr. Angel said. "The rules are strict. The first is that the person must want to find the property very badly. The second is that the person must have tried as hard as he possibly could to find it. Third, it must be property that is intended for someone else."

"All that is true about Albert," Lucille said.

"I know," said Mr. Angel. "That is why I have arranged for him to claim his property. It is a small gold medallion on a fine gold chain, is it not?"

"It was the only one I could get," Albert said.

"Then follow me," said Mr. Angel.

They moved past shelves of found wallets, found passports, found walking sticks, found photographs, every kind of found article. At last they came to the Department of Found Jewelry.

"Here we are," Mr. Angel said. "This is your medallion."

"Are you sure?" said Albert. "It looks quite different." It was much more neatly wrapped than Albert remembered, and in much more suitable paper.

"Perfectly sure," Mr. Angel said.

"Then thank you," Albert said. "Lucille and I are very grateful."

"Not at all, not at all," said Mr. Angel. "And now you must leave. We have other places to visit."

Albert, Lucille, and Redvers stepped out of the barn. The door closed behind them, and the magical radiance died away. All that was left was an old barn in a vacant lot.

Savage cold crept back with the darkness. It came with a steely wind. Albert felt it on his legs, on his ears, his nose, the skin of his cheeks.

"Let's go," said Redvers. He took Lucille in his left hand. With his right he held Albert by the arm, and suddenly they were off.

"We're flying, Lucille," cried Albert. "I think we're flying!"

"My eyes are closed," Lucille said. "My eyes are shut tight. I am a dog, not a bird. Don't look down."

But Albert did look down. He saw below him the white roofs of the houses, the roads empty of traffic. The whole town was sleeping. It was early Christmas morning.

They flew through the hushed darkness. They flew down Albert's street. Gently as a snowflake, Redvers delivered them at the door of Albert's house.

The whole flight had taken but a minute.

"Do you have that present safe?" asked Redvers.

"Oh yes," said Albert. "It's in my hand."

"In you go," Redvers said.

Albert opened the door. He turned to thank Redvers.

Redvers was nowhere to be seen. He had left no foot-prints in the snow. There was no sign that he had ever been.

"Let's go in," Lucille said. "I'm so cold."

They fell into bed and slept at once.

It was daylight when Albert awoke. A pale cold lemon-colored sun shone through his window. It was daylight on Christmas morning.

"Wake up," Albert said to Lucille. "It's late and it's Christmas."

"I am awake," Lucille said. "At least, I think I'm awake. I think my eyes are open. It's hard to tell."

"You're under the covers, that's why you can't see," explained Albert. "Come on. It's time to get up."

Albert went to the bathroom and washed up. He thought about the night's adventures.

"Do you think it was a dream?" he asked Lucille.

"Certainly not," Lucille said. "Just look on your table."

There, neat and shapely and elegantly wrapped, was the small package that held the medallion.

Albert picked it up. It was certainly real. "I have to give it to Mom," said Albert.

"Naturally, naturally," said Lucille.

They went downstairs.

Albert's father was in the living room. On his feet he wore a new pair of blue leather slippers. "What do you think?" he said to Albert.

Albert looked at the slippers. He liked them. "Nice," he said.

"A Christmas present from your mother," Albert's father said. "When are you going to look at your presents?"

"Later," Albert said. "It's important that I see Mom right away."

"Urgent," said Lucille. "Critical."

"She's in the kitchen," Albert's father said. "I'll come with you, since it's important."

Holding the present tightly, Albert led the way into the kitchen. His mother sat at the breakfast table. She was eating toast and marmalade, which she liked very much.

"Good morning, Albert," she said. "Merry Christmas."

"This is for you, Mom," said Albert. He gave her the small package.

"Why, Albert," she said, "this is the most beautiful package I've ever seen. It seems a pity to open it."

"You can open it," Albert said, "if you want to." He was quite nervous.

His mother took her scissors. Carefully she unwrapped the box. She didn't tear even a small corner of the paper. She held the box in her hand and removed the lid. "What can it be?" she said. "Albert, what do we have here?"

Albert couldn't speak. It certainly didn't look like the box he'd bought. It was beautiful.

Gently his mother took away the soft, white paper from within the box. Then she took out a small, round gold medallion on a delicate gold chain. The little medallion hung from her fingers on its chain.

She turned to Albert. "This can't be," she said. "This is my own medallion. Look, here's the Christmas tree on its face. And here, on the back—here's my name. Helen Lavinia O'Keefe!" Her face was radiant.

Albert was stunned.

"Oh," said Albert's mother, "how did this happen? Where did you get it?"

"I don't know how it happened," Albert said. "An angel gave it to me."

His mother looked at him very closely.

"Remarkable," said his father. "Quite remarkable."

"I don't know much about angels," Albert's mother

said, "but I think you must be an angel, Albert." Her eyes were shining.

"Heh, heh!" said Lucille, who was under the table looking for scraps of fallen toast. "Some angel! Heh, heh!"

Albert ignored Lucille. "I'm glad you have it back, Mom," he said. He hugged his mother hard. "Merry Christmas, Mom."

After breakfast, Albert and Lucille opened their presents. Some were expected and some were surprises. All were perfect.

Then Albert dressed, and they went into the yard. The lawn was covered with untouched snow. Not even a bird had marked the surface with the frail twigs of its feet.

Albert turned to face the house, spread his arms wide, and fell backward into the snow. It was soft and deep. Vigorously, he flapped his arms and opened and closed his legs.

When he got up, he left behind a clear shape. "Look," he said to Lucille, "I've made a snow angel."

"So you have," said Lucille. "Watch me." She rolled and wriggled and kicked about in the snow.

They stood together and examined their angels.

"Your snow angel," Lucille said, "looks like an angel. It has wings and is rather lovely. Mine looks terrible."

"It looks like a doughnut angel," said Albert.

"Or a bagel angel," said Lucille.

"Or a sausage angel," said Albert. "Actually, I think it looks exactly like a dog angel."

"Thank you," said Lucille.

They scampered about in the white yard, and little puffs and clouds of snow rose round about them.

Albert and Lucille were perfectly happy.

For Kitty —L.N.
For Susan, the angel in my life —M.G.

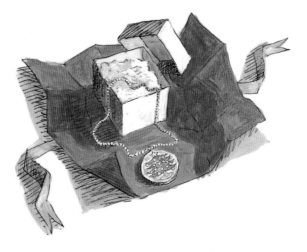

The author thanks his friend Richard Parkinson
for encouraging him to write this story.

Text copyright © 2000 by Leslie Norris
Illustrations copyright © 2000 by Mordicai Gerstein
All rights reserved
Distributed in Canada by Douglas & McIntyre Ltd.
Color separations by Hong Kong Scanner Arts
Printed and bound in the United States of America by Worzalla
Designed by Judy Lanfredi
First edition, 2000

Library of Congress Cataloging-in-Publication Data
Norris, Leslie.
    Albert and the angels / Leslie Norris ; pictures by Mordicai Gerstein. — 1st ed.
        p.   cm.
    Summary: As Christmas approaches, a young boy and his talking dog, which
only he can hear, try their best to find a replacement for the special medallion
that his mother lost long ago.
    ISBN 0-374-30192-1
    [1. Christmas—Fiction.   2. Lost and found possessions—Fiction.
3. Dogs—Fiction. 4. Angels—Fiction.] I. Gerstein, Mordicai, ill. II. Title.
PZ7.N7923A1   2000
[Fic]—dc21   98-36184